Macbeth

THE GRAPHIC NOVEL
William Shakespeare

PLAIN TEXT VERSION

Script Adaptation: John McDonald
Character Designs & Original Artwork: Jon Haward
Colouring & Lettering: Nigel Do
Inking Assistant: Gary Erskine

Design & Layout: Jo Wheeler
Additional Information: Karen Wenborn

Editor in Chief: Clive Bryant

Macbeth: The Graphic Novel
Plain Text Version

William Shakespeare

First UK Edition

Published by: Classical Comics Ltd
Copyright ©2008 Classical Comics Ltd.

Acknowledgments: Every effort has been made to trace copyright holders of
material reproduced in this book. Any rights not acknowledged here will be
acknowledged in subsequent editions if notice is given to Classical Comics Ltd.

Images on pages 3 & 6 reproduced with the kind permission of
the Trustees of the National Library of Scotland. © National Library of Scotland.

All enquiries should be addressed to:
Classical Comics Ltd.
PO Box 7280
Litchborough
Towcester
NN12 9AR
United Kingdom
Tel: 0845 812 3000

info@classicalcomics.com
www.classicalcomics.com

ISBN: 978-1-906332-04-4

Printed in the UK by Hampton Printing (Bristol) Ltd
using biodegradable vegetable inks on environmentally friendly paper.
This material can be disposed of by recycling,
incineration for energy recovery, composting and biodegradation.

The rights of John McDonald, Jon Haward, Nigel Dobbyn and Gary Erskine
to be identified as the artists of this work have been asserted in accordance with
the Copyright, Designs and Patents Act 1988 sections 77 and 78.

Contents

Dramatis Personæ

Duncan
King of Scotland

Malcolm
Son of Duncan

Donalbain
Son of Duncan

Macduff
Nobleman of Scotland

Lenox
Nobleman of Scotland

Rosse
Nobleman of Scotland

Lady Macbeth
Wife of Macbeth

Lady Macduff
Wife of Macduff

Siward *Earl of Northumberland,*
General of the English forces

**A Gentlewoman attending
to Lady Macbeth**

Seyton
An officer attending to Macbeth

An English Doctor

A Scottish Doctor

A Porter

An Old Man

Murderer 1

Murderer 2

Murderer 3

Dramatis Personæ

Macbeth
General in the King's Army

Banquo
General in the King's Army

The Ghost of Banquo

Menteth
Nobleman of Scotland

Angus
Nobleman of Scotland

Cathness
Nobleman of Scotland

Young Siward
Son of Siward

Fleance
Son of Banquo

Boy
Son of Macduff

Witch 1

Witch 2

Witch 3

Hecate
The "Queen" Witch

and Lords, Ladies,
Officers, Soldiers,
Messengers, Attendants
and Apparitions.

Prologue

Scotland in the year 1040.

King Duncan has ruled the land for six years, ever since the death of his grandfather, Malcolm II. Duncan is a good king, but even under his kind and gentle ruling, Scotland is far from being a settled nation.

For centuries, following the departure of the Romans, the land has been split in two — with bands of Vikings in the north, and tribes of Saxons in the south. It's a barbaric land. Each local tribe has its own strong leader: men relying on the strength of their sword arm for honours and often having to fight for their very survival.

But the country is changing. With the reign of King Duncan came a rare promise of unity amongst the tribes to create a single, Scottish nation ruled by a single Scottish King. However, not everyone welcomes this peace. Some chieftains want to maintain their independence and continue to rebel against the King, often joining forces with warriors from other tribes and from other countries such as Ireland and Norway; and there are even some chieftains who would like to claim the title of King of Scotland for themselves.

To defend his crown, and to maintain order in his land, King Duncan commands a powerful army, led by noblemen who are experienced in the ways of war - and the mightiest and most trusted of these noblemen is King Duncan's cousin, the Thane of Glamis, otherwise known as...

...Macbeth.

In his camp at Forres, King Duncan receives news of his army's battle against a rebellion...

WHO IS THIS MAN COVERED IN *BLOOD?* HE LOOKS LIKE HE CAN GIVE US THE *LATEST NEWS* FROM THE *BATTLEFIELD.*

THIS SERGEANT FOUGHT LIKE A *REAL SOLDIER* TO SAVE ME FROM BEING *CAPTURED.*

GREETINGS, MY BRAVE FRIEND!

TELL THE KING HOW THINGS *STAND.*

IT WAS POISED ON A *KNIFE-EDGE.* BOTH ARMIES WERE EXHAUSTED AND DEADLOCKED. THAT HEARTLESS EVIL REBEL, *MACDONWALD,* BROUGHT IN *REINFORCEMENTS* FROM THE *WESTERN ISLES.*

THAT'S WHEN THINGS BEGAN TO *GO HIS WAY* AND FORTUNE *SMILED* ON HIM LIKE A *REBEL'S*

BUT IT DIDN'T *LAST* -- BECAUSE BRAVE *MACBETH* NEGLECTED HIS OWN SAFETY AND CARVED HIS WAY THROUGH THEM WITH A *BLOODY, SMOKING* SWORD -- UNTIL HE *FACED* MACDONWALD.

HE DIDN'T STOP TO SHAKE HANDS OR SAY GOODBYE -- HE JUST *RIPPED* THE VILLAIN FROM *NAVEL* TO *JAW* AND STUCK HIS *HEAD* ON OUR *BATTLEMENTS.*

FROM *FIFE*, GREAT KING; WHERE THE *NORWEGIAN BANNERS* HAVE BEEN FLYING FREELY. THE NORWEGIAN KING HIMSELF, ALONG WITH A *HUGE ARMY*, HELPED BY THAT DISLOYAL TRAITOR, *THE THANE OF CAWDOR*, BEGAN A *TERRIBLE ASSAULT*.

THEN *MACBETH* FEARLESSLY CONFRONTED HIM HEAD-ON AND MATCHED HIM BLOW FOR BLOW IN SINGLE COMBAT -- UNTIL HE FINALLY *GAVE IN* -- AND *VICTORY* WAS *OURS*.

GREAT *NEWS!*

THE NORWEGIAN KING WANTED TO NEGOTIATE *TERMS*, BUT WE WOULDN'T ALLOW HIM TO BURY HIS MEN UNTIL HE PAID US *TEN THOUSAND DOLLARS* AT *SAINT COLME'S INCH*.

THE THANE OF CAWDOR MUST NEVER BE ALLOWED TO TURN AGAINST US AGAIN. GO SEE TO HIS *IMMEDIATE EXECUTION* AND GIVE HIS *TITLE* TO *MACBETH*.

I'LL MAKE SURE IT'S DONE.

WHAT HE HAS *LOST*, NOBLE MACBETH HAS *WON*.

A Scottish heath...

WHERE HAVE YOU BEEN, SISTER?

KILLING SWINE.

WHAT ABOUT YOU, SISTER?

A SAILOR'S WIFE HAD **CHESTNUTS** IN HER LAP, AND MUNCHED AND MUNCHED AND MUNCHED:

"GIVE ME," SAID I: "GO AWAY, WITCH!" THE RUMP-FED CREATURE CRIED.

HER HUSBAND'S GONE TO **ALEPPO**, THE MASTER OF A **SHIP:** BUT IN A **SIEVE** I'M GOING TO SAIL, AND, LIKE A RAT WITHOUT A TAIL; I'LL DO, I'LL DO AND I'LL DO.

I'LL GIVE YOU A WIND.

YOU'RE KIND.

AND I ANOTHER.

15

WE'LL GO FROM HERE TO *INVERNESS*, SO WE CAN VISIT YOUR *CASTLE* AND BECOME *CLOSER* FRIENDS.

IT WILL BE MY *PLEASURE*. I'LL ACT AS MESSENGER *MYSELF* AND CARRY THE GOOD NEWS TO MY *WIFE*. SO, KINDLY ALLOW ME TO TAKE MY LEAVE.

THE *PRINCE OF CUMBERLAND?* THAT OBSTACLE'S IN MY WAY AND COULD *TRIP* ME UP... UNLESS I *JUMP OVER* IT. STARS, HIDE YOUR FIRE...

AND DON'T LET ANY LIGHT SHINE ON MY *DARK* AND DEEP *DESIRE*. MY EYES PREFER NOT TO SEE WHAT MY HAND MIGHT DO. NEVERTHELESS... LET IT BE DONE.

WHAT AN HONOURABLE MAN YOU ARE!

IT'S *TRUE*, BANQUO, HE REALLY IS A GREAT MAN AND IT MAKES ME *HAPPY* TO SAY THAT. PRAISING HIM IS LIKE A *BANQUET* TO ME.

LET'S GET AFTER HIM. HE IS SO *CONSCIENTIOUS*, HE'S RACED ON AHEAD TO PREPARE OUR *WELCOME*.

Act One
Scene Five

At Macbeth's castle, in Inverness, Lady Macbeth receives news from her husband...

"THEY MET ME ON THE DAY OF *VICTORY*, AND I'VE FOUND OUT THEY HAVE *SUPERNATURAL INSIGHT*.

WHEN I TRIED TO QUESTION THEM *FURTHER*, THEY *VANISHED* INTO THIN AIR."

"AND, WHILE I WAS STANDING THERE MESMERISED, MESSENGERS CAME FROM THE KING, CALLING ME *THANE OF CAWDOR*. THIS IS THE TITLE THE WEIRD SISTERS HAD ONLY JUST *GIVEN* ME, AND THEY ALSO REFERRED TO THE FUTURE WITH *HAIL, KING THAT SHALL BE!*"

"I HAD TO DELIVER THIS NEWS TO YOU, MY DEAREST PARTNER OF GREATNESS, SO YOU WOULDN'T LOSE A SECOND OF PLEASURE THROUGH NOT KNOWING WHAT'S BEEN *PROMISED* TO YOU. HOLD IT TO YOUR *HEART* AND FAREWELL."

YOU *ARE* GLAMIS, AND CAWDOR NOW! AND YOU'LL BECOME WHAT HAS BEEN *PROMISED* TO YOU. I'M JUST AFRAID YOUR NATURE IS TOO FULL OF THE *MILK OF HUMAN KINDNESS* TO DO WHAT'S NECESSARY. YOU WANT TO BE *GREAT* -- YOU'RE *AMBITIOUS* -- YOU JUST LACK THE *RUTHLESSNESS* IT TAKES TO *GET* THERE.

YOU ALWAYS WANT TO ACT *HONOURABLY* TO GET WHAT YOU DESIRE. YOU WON'T *DOUBLE-DEAL*, BUT YOU STILL LIKE TO WIN WHICHEVER WAY YOU *CAN*. BUT NOW YOU WANT THE THING THAT CAN ONLY BE ACHIEVED BY CERTAIN POSITIVE ACTIONS... ACTIONS YOU'RE *AFRAID* TO CARRY OUT, RATHER THAN ACTIONS YOU'D *REGRET*.

COME *HOME* TO ME, SO I CAN POUR MY *SPIRIT* INTO YOUR EAR AND *EXPEL*, WITH THE SINCERITY OF MY WORDS, ALL IMPEDIMENTS TO THE GOLDEN FUTURE THAT *FATE* AND *SUPERNATURAL ASSISTANCE* SEEM TO HAVE IN STORE FOR US.

GREAT THANE OF GLAMIS! DESERVING THANE OF CAWDOR! GREATER THAN *BOTH*... ACCORDING TO PROPHESY!

YOUR *LETTER'S* TAKEN ME *BEYOND* THE IMMEDIATE PRESENT AND *EVEN NOW* I CAN FEEL THE *FUTURE*.

MY DEAREST LOVE, *DUNCAN'S* COMING HERE TONIGHT.

AND WHEN IS HE LEAVING?

HE INTENDS TO LEAVE *TOMORROW*.

HE'LL NEVER *SEE* TOMORROW! MY THANE, YOUR *FACE* IS LIKE A *BOOK* WHERE *ANYONE* CAN READ WHAT'S IN YOUR HEART. YOU'LL HAVE TO *LIGHTEN UP* TO *MISLEAD* THEM. YOUR *HANDSHAKE* AND YOUR *VOICE*... YOUR *WELCOME*, ALL HAVE TO APPEAR *GENUINE*. YOU'LL HAVE TO LOOK AS INNOCENT AS A *FLOWER*...

...A FLOWER THAT'S HIDING A *SERPENT*. DUNCAN HAS TO BE *WINED AND DINED*. YOU CAN LEAVE THE *REAL* BUSINESS OF THE NIGHT TO *ME*...

...BUSINESS THAT WILL SHAPE THE *REST OF OUR LIVES*.

WE'LL TALK ABOUT IT LATER.

JUST BE *CLEAR* IN YOUR MIND... DON'T *REGRET* THIS CHANCE FOREVER. LEAVE THE REST TO *ME*.

LOOK! OUR HONOURABLE **HOSTESS!** THEY LOVE US SO MUCH AND GO TO SUCH GREAT LENGTHS TO MAKE US WELCOME. THIS IS HOW GUESTS **SHOULD** BE GREETED AND I REALLY **APPRECIATE** IT.

DOUBLE **EVERYTHING** WE CAN DO, THEN DOUBLE IT AGAIN -- AND IT **STILL** WOULDN'T BE ENOUGH TO SHOW OUR GRATITUDE FOR THE GREAT **HONOURS** YOUR MAJESTY HAS BESTOWED UPON US. WE'RE DEEPLY IN YOUR DEBT FOR EVERYTHING YOU'VE GIVEN US IN THE PAST, AND NOW FOR THIS **NEW** PRESTIGE AS WELL.

WHERE **IS** THE THANE OF CAWDOR? WE TRIED HARD TO CATCH UP WITH HIM, BUT HE RIDES SO **FAST.**

BUT THEN, HE HAS SO **MUCH** TO RACE **HOME** FOR. LOVELY AND NOBLE HOSTESS, WE ARE YOUR **GUEST** TONIGHT.

WE ARE YOUR SERVANTS **FOREVER.** EVERYTHING IN OUR HOME IS **YOURS.**

GIVE ME YOUR HAND. TAKE ME TO MY HOST. WE LOVE HIM MOST DEARLY AND WE SHALL **CONTINUE** OUR FAVOURS TO HIM. IF YOU **PLEASE,** HOSTESS.

Act One Scene Seven

An evening banquet in honour of the King...

25

STOP! LEAVE ME ALONE! I'M NOT AFRAID TO DO *ANYTHING* THAT BEFITS A *MAN* -- BUT ANYONE WHO DARES TO DO *MORE* THAN THAT IS AN *ANIMAL!*

WHAT *ANIMAL* MADE YOU BREAK YOUR *PROMISE* TO ME? WHEN YOU DARED TO DO IT, *THEN* YOU WERE A *MAN*. AND, IF YOU WERE *KING*, YOU'D BE EVEN *MORE* OF A MAN. TIME AND PLACE DIDN'T *MATTER* THEN, BUT NOW YOU'RE MAKING *EXCUSES*.

NOW THERE IS NOTHING *BUT* EXCUSES AND THAT WILL BE YOUR *UNDOING*.

I HAVE *BREAST FED*, AND I KNOW HOW *TENDER* A THING IT IS TO LOVE THE BABY THAT TAKES *MILK* FROM ME. YET, I'D RATHER PULL MY *NIPPLE* FROM HIS GUMS AND BASH HIS *BRAINS* OUT, THAN *BREAK A PROMISE* I'D MADE TO *YOU!*

WHAT IF WE *FAIL?*

THEN WE FAIL! BUT IF YOU KEEP YOUR *NERVE*, WE *WON'T* FAIL.

WHEN DUNCAN'S *ASLEEP,* WHICH SHOULDN'T TAKE *LONG* AFTER THE *JOURNEY* HE'S HAD, I'LL MAKE SURE HIS TWO *ATTENDANTS* ARE *SO DRUNK* THAT THEY WON'T BE ABLE TO REMEMBER A *THING.* AND, WHEN THEY'RE SLEEPING LIKE PIGS, IN THEIR *DRUNKEN STATE,* WE CAN DO WHAT WE *LIKE* TO THE *UNGUARDED DUNCAN.*

AND WE CAN BLAME IT ALL ON THE *DRUNKEN GUARDS* WHO'LL BE MADE *GUILTY* FOR WHAT *WE* DO.

GIVE *BIRTH TO BOYS ONLY!* BECAUSE YOUR *RESOLUTE STRENGTH* SHOULD MAKE NOTHING BUT *MALES.*

IT HAS TO BE BELIEVED THAT HIS *OWN PEOPLE* DID IT, SO WE'LL USE *THEIR DAGGERS* AND SMEAR THEIR BODIES WITH HIS *BLOOD.*

WHO'D DARE BELIEVE *ANYTHING ELSE,* AFTER THE SHOW OF *OUTRAGE* AND *GRIEF* WE'LL MAKE ABOUT HIS *DEATH?*

I'M *READY.* MY *WHOLE BODY* IS READY TO DO THIS. LET'S GET BACK AND PUT ON OUR *ACT.* OUR *FACES* HAVE TO HIDE WHAT'S IN OUR *HEARTS.*

YOU DID *WELL.* I *DREAMT* ABOUT THE THREE *WEIRD SISTERS* LAST NIGHT. THEY'VE SHOWN *YOU* SOME *TRUTH.*

I DON'T *THINK* ABOUT THEM. MAYBE, WHEN WE'VE AN HOUR TO SPARE, WE SHOULD *TALK* ABOUT THAT BUSINESS... IF YOU *WANT* TO.

WHATEVER SUITS YOU.

IF YOU CAN WAIT 'TIL I'M *READY...* I'D *APPRECIATE* IT.

AS LONG AS I LOSE *NO OTHER* RESPECT AND AS LONG AS MY *CONSCIENCE* STAYS CLEAR, I'LL *LISTEN* TO YOU.

IN THE MEANTIME, *SLEEP WELL!*

THANKS SIR, THE SAME TO YOU!

31

32

Act Two
Scene Two

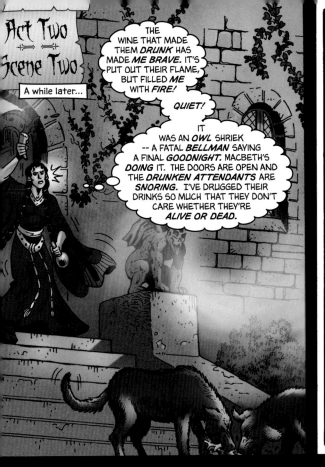

A while later...

THE WINE THAT MADE THEM *DRUNK* HAS MADE *ME* BRAVE. IT'S PUT OUT THEIR FLAME, BUT FILLED *ME* WITH *FIRE!*

QUIET!

IT WAS AN *OWL* SHRIEK -- A FATAL *BELLMAN* SAYING A FINAL *GOODNIGHT.* MACBETH'S *DOING* IT. THE DOORS ARE OPEN AND THE *DRUNKEN ATTENDANTS* ARE *SNORING.* I'VE DRUGGED THEIR DRINKS SO MUCH THAT THEY DON'T CARE WHETHER THEY'RE *ALIVE OR DEAD.*

WHO'S THERE? WHO IS IT?

OH NO! THEY MUST HAVE *WOKEN* AND IT *HASN'T BEEN DONE.* WE'VE BEEN CAUGHT IN THE ACT -- *LISTEN!* -- I LEFT THE *DAGGERS* READY FOR HIM... HE COULDN'T *MISS* THEM. IF DUNCAN HADN'T LOOKED LIKE MY *FATHER* IN HIS SLEEP, I'D HAVE DONE IT *MYSELF.*

MY *HUSBAND!*

I'VE *DONE* IT. DID YOU HEAR A *NOISE?*

I HEARD AN *OWL* SCREAM AND THE *CRICKETS* CRY. DID YOU NOT *SPEAK?*

ONE SHOUTED *"GOD BLESS US!"* AND THE OTHER ANSWERED *"AMEN"*... AS IF THEY'D *SEEN* ME WITH THESE *MURDERER'S HANDS.* I COULD HEAR THEIR *FEAR,* BUT I COULDN'T SAY *"AMEN"* WHEN THEY SAID *"GOD BLESS US".*

DON'T *WORRY* ABOUT IT.

BUT WHY COULDN'T I SAY *"AMEN"?* I NEEDED A *BLESSING* AND *"AMEN" STUCK* IN MY *THROAT.*

IF WE KEEP *DWELLING* ON IT, IT'LL DRIVE US *MAD.*

I THOUGHT I HEARD A *VOICE* SHOUT OUT *"SLEEP NO MORE! MACBETH IS MURDERING SLEEP".*

INNOCENT SLEEP... SLEEP, THAT TAKES AWAY ALL OUR *WORRIES,* THE END OF EACH DAY'S *TROUBLE,* HARD WORK'S *RELIEF, SOOTHER* OF *DAMAGED MINDS,* NATURE'S *SECOND CHANCE,* CHIEF NOURISHER IN *LIFE'S FEAST...*

WHAT *ARE* YOU *TALKING* ABOUT?

IT KEPT SHOUTING *"SLEEP NO MORE!",* ALL OVER THE CASTLE. *"GLAMIS* HAS *MURDERED* SLEEP, SO *CAWDOR* WILL SLEEP *NO MORE; MACBETH* WILL SLEEP *NO MORE!".*

35

MY **HANDS** ARE THE SAME COLOUR AS **YOURS,** BUT I'D BE **ASHAMED** TO HAVE A **HEART** AS **WHITE.**

BANG! BANG!

THERE'S SOMEONE **KNOCKING** AT THE **SOUTH** ENTRY. LET'S GET TO OUR **ROOM.** A LITTLE **WATER** WILL WASH AWAY THIS CRIME. IT'S **EASY.** IT'S YOUR **LOYALTY** THAT'S MAKING YOU VULNERABLE.

BANG! BANG!

LISTEN! MORE KNOCKING. PUT ON YOUR **NIGHTGOWN,** IN CASE WE'RE **CALLED** UPON AND WE'RE SEEN TO BE **WATCHING.** AND DON'T BE SO DISTRACTED BY YOUR **CONSCIENCE.**

IT'D BE BETTER NOT TO KNOW **MYSELF,** THAN TO KNOW WHAT I'VE **DONE.**

BANG! BANG!

WAKE **DUNCAN** WITH YOUR KNOCKING... I WISH YOU COULD!

WHY SIR, IT MAKES YOUR *NOSE RED*, MAKES YOU *SLEEP* AND MAKES YOU *URINATE*. *LUST* SIR, IT *ENCOURAGES* AND *DISCOURAGES*. IT *ENCOURAGES* THE *DESIRE*, BUT *DISCOURAGES* THE *PERFORMANCE*.

SO, DRINK CAN BE SAID TO BE A *HYPOCRITE* WHEN IT COMES TO *LUST*. IT *MAKES* IT AND *BREAKS* IT. IT TURNS IT *ON* AND TURNS IT *OFF*. IT MAKES IT *STAND UP* AND *LIE DOWN*. IN SHORT, IT *LIES* TO LUST.

I'D SAY THE *DRINK* LIED TO *YOU* LAST NIGHT.

IT CERTAINLY *DID* SIR, THROUGH ITS *TEETH*. BUT I GOT EVEN. I RECKON I WAS *TOO STRONG* FOR IT BECAUSE, EVEN THOUGH IT TOOK MY *LEGS* AWAY, I *THREW IT BACK*.

OUR *KNOCKING* MUST HAVE *DISTURBED* HIM. HERE HE COMES.

GOOD *MORNING*, NOBLE SIR!

GOOD *MORNING* TO YOU BOTH.

IS YOUR *MASTER* AWAKE?

IS THE *KING* UP YET, HONOURABLE THANE?

NOT YET.

HE ORDERED ME TO CALL HIM *EARLY*. I WAS VERY NEARLY *LATE*.

39

41

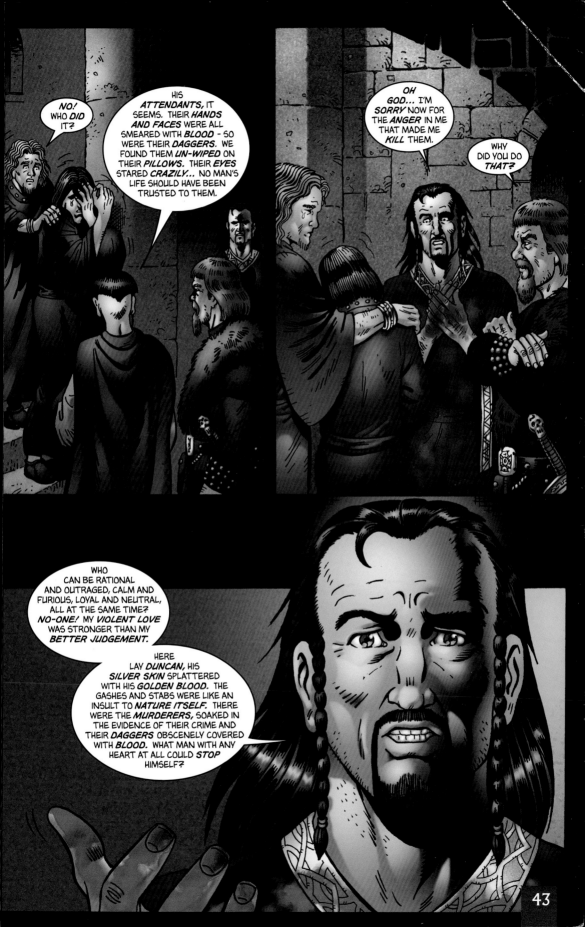

43

44

LET'S QUICKLY *GET READY* AND MEET UP AGAIN IN THE *GREAT HALL*.

AYE!

LET'S NOT JOIN THEM. IT'LL BE EASY FOR THE PERPETRATOR TO CRY *CROCODILE TEARS* AND GET THE *REST* OF THEM ON HIS *SIDE*. I'LL GO TO *ENGLAND*. WHAT WILL *YOU* DO?

I'LL GO TO *IRELAND*. IT'S BETTER IF WE *SPLIT UP*. WE CAN'T STAY HERE. THERE'S *DANGER* IN *MEN'S SMILES*. AND THE CLOSER THE *RELATIVE*, THE GREATER THE *DANGER*.

THE *MURDEROUS ARROW* THAT'S BEEN RELEASED HASN'T YET FALLEN TO *GROUND*. OUR SAFEST BET IS TO *GET OUT OF ITS WAY*. SO, LET'S FIND OUR *HORSES* AS QUICKLY AS WE CAN AND NOT BE TOO CONCERNED WITH *SAYING GOODBYE*. OUR DANGEROUS SITUATION *JUSTIFIES* OUR *QUICK DEPARTURE*.

45

Act Two
Scene Four

Later that day, outside Macbeth's castle, the Thane of Rosse meets with an old man...

GOOD FATHER, YOU CAN SEE THE *HEAVENS* ARE *ANGRY* ABOUT WHAT'S BEEN DONE HERE ON EARTH. THEY TURN *DAY* INTO *NIGHT*. IT SHOULD BE *BRIGHT*, BUT *DARKNESS* COVERS THE SUN. MAYBE THE DAYLIGHT'S *ASHAMED* TO SHOW ITS FACE AND THAT'S WHY IT ALLOWS THE *NIGHT* TO BURY THE EARTH IN *SHADOW*.

I CAN REMEMBER BACK *SEVENTY YEARS* -- AND I'VE SEEN SOME *STRANGE THINGS* IN THAT TIME -- BUT *NOTHING* AS TERRIBLE AS *LAST NIGHT*.

IT'S *UNNATURAL*, JUST LIKE THAT BUSINESS UP THERE. LAST TUESDAY, A HIGH-FLYING *FALCON* WAS HUNTED AND KILLED BY A MOUSING *OWL*.

AND HERE'S SOMETHING *ELSE* THAT'S STRANGE BUT TRUE... DUNCAN'S *HORSES*, THE MOST *PERFECT EXAMPLES OF THEIR BREED*, WENT *WILD* AND BROKE OUT OF THEIR *STALLS*. THEY COULDN'T BE *CONTROLLED* -- IT WAS LIKE THEY WERE *POSSESSED* BY SOME *DEMON* THAT *HATED MANKIND*.

THEY SAY THEY *ATE* EACH OTHER.

THEY *DID*. I *SAW* IT WITH MY *OWN EYES*.

HERE COMES *MACDUFF*.

46

47

Act Three Scene One

Macbeth is now King of Scotland. In the King's Palace at Forres, Banquo is suspicious...

YOU HAVE IT *ALL... KING, CAWDOR, GLAMIS, EVERYTHING.* JUST AS THE *WEIRD WOMEN* PROMISED. BUT, I SUSPECT YOU HAVEN'T PLAYED *FAIR* TO *GET* IT. STILL, THEY SAID IT WON'T *STAY* IN YOUR FAMILY AND THAT I'LL BE THE *FATHER* OF *MANY KINGS.* IF THEY TOLD *YOU* THE TRUTH, THEN WHY SHOULDN'T I HOPE THEIR PROPHESIES WILL COME TRUE FOR *ME?*

HUSH; NO MORE!

TAN-TARA!

TAN-TARA!

AH, OUR *CHIEF GUEST'S* HERE.

IT WOULD BE *BAD MANNERS* TO *FORGET* HIM -- OUR *GREAT FEAST* WOULDN'T BE COMPLETE *WITHOUT* HIM.

WE'RE HOLDING A *FORMAL BANQUET* TONIGHT, SIR. AND I'LL EXPECT YOU TO *BE* THERE.

YOUR *COMMANDS* AND *MY DUTIES* ARE LINKED TOGETHER WITH AN *UNBREAKABLE BOND...* FOREVER.

ARE YOU GOING OUT *RIDING* THIS AFTERNOON?

YES, I AM.

I'D HAVE VALUED YOUR *GOOD ADVICE* IN TODAY'S *COUNCIL MEETING*; BUT *TOMORROW* WILL DO. ARE YOU RIDING *FAR*?

DON'T MISS OUR *BANQUET.*

I *WON'T,* MY LORD.

AS *FAR,* MY LORD, AS I CAN BETWEEN *NOW* AND *SUPPER* -- UNLESS MY *HORSE* LETS ME DOWN, IN WHICH CASE I MIGHT BE BACK AN HOUR OR TWO AFTER NIGHTFALL.

WE HEAR *DUNCAN'S SONS* ARE *HIDING* IN *ENGLAND* AND *IRELAND,* REFUSING TO ADMIT TO THE CRUEL KILLING OF THEIR FATHER. THEY'RE TELLING *OUTRAGEOUS LIES* TO ANYONE WHO'LL LISTEN. BUT MORE ON THAT TOMORROW, WHEN WE GET A CHANCE TO DISCUSS *MATTERS OF STATE* TOGETHER.

GO TO YOUR HORSE. *FAREWELL...* UNTIL TONIGHT.

IS *FLEANCE* GOING WITH YOU?

YES, MY LORD. HE'S *WAITING* FOR ME.

MAY YOUR HORSES BE *SWIFT AND STEADY.* HAVE A *SAFE RIDE.*

FAREWELL.

EVERYONE... USE YOUR TIME AS YOU *PLEASE* UNTIL *SEVEN TONIGHT.* TO BE IN THE BEST FORM FOR SOCIALISING, WE'LL SPEND THE AFTERNOON *ALONE.* UNTIL THEN, *GOD BE WITH YOU.*

ARE THOSE *MEN* HERE?

THEY *ARE,* MY LORD, OUTSIDE THE PALACE GATE.

BRING THEM TO ME.

TO BE *KING* IS *NOTHING.* TO *STAY* KING... *THAT'S* WHAT MATTERS. MY FEAR OF *BANQUO* RUNS *DEEP.* IT'S HIS *NATURAL NOBILITY* THAT'S SO THREATENING.

HE'S AFRAID OF *NOTHING,* BUT HE'S ALSO *CLEVER* ENOUGH ONLY TO ACT WHEN THE *TIME'S RIGHT.* HE'S THE ONLY ONE I'M *AFRAID* OF AND, BESIDE HIM, MY *REPUTATION'S DIMINISHED* -- JUST LIKE *MARK ANTHONY'S* WAS BY CAESAR.

HE *REPROACHED* THE WITCHES WHEN THEY FIRST GAVE ME THE NAME OF *"KING".* HE INSISTED THEY SPEAK TO *HIM.* AND, WHEN THEY *DID,* THEY SAID HE'D BE *FATHER* TO A *LINE OF KINGS.*

51

53

NOW, IF **YOU** HAVE A PLACE IN THE RECORD BOOKS, ABOVE THE VERY WORST CLASS OF HUMAN, **SAY** IT! AND I'LL PUT SOME **BUSINESS** YOUR WAY THAT'LL TAKE CARE OF YOUR **ENEMY** AND **ENDEAR** YOU TO ME. MY **OWN HEALTH** IS AFFECTED BY HIS LIFE AND ONLY HIS **DEATH** WILL **CURE** ME.

I'M SO **INCENSED** BY THE WORLD, MY LIEGE, THAT I DON'T CARE **WHAT** I DO TO **SPITE** IT.

SAME. I'M **SO TIRED** OF **HARDSHIP** AND **BAD LUCK** THAT I'D DO **ANYTHING** TO CHANGE MY LIFE, OR ELSE BE **RID** OF IT.

I'M THE

BOTH OF YOU KNOW THAT **BANQUO** IS YOUR **ENEMY.**

YES, MY LORD.

HE'S MINE **TOO** -- SO MUCH SO THAT EVERY MINUTE HE **LIVES** IS LIKE A **KNIFE-WOUND** IN MY HEART.

I COULD SWEEP HIM AWAY WITH **BRUTE FORCE** IF I WANTED TO, BUT I **MUSTN'T.** WE HAVE SOME **MUTUAL FRIENDS** I DON'T WANT TO **LOSE.** THEY'D TAKE **OFFENCE** IF I STRUCK HIM DOWN **MYSELF.** THAT'S WHY I'VE COME TO **YOU** FOR HELP. IT HAS TO BE DONE **SECRETLY,** FOR **LOTS** OF REASONS.

WE'LL DO WHATEVER YOU **SAY,** MY LORD.

EVEN THOUGH OUR **LIVES...**

YOUR **COURAGE** IS OUTSTANDING.

DUNCAN'S IN HIS *GRAVE*. HE SLEEPS *SOUNDLY* NOW, AFTER ALL THE TRIALS OF LIFE. *TREASON* HAS DONE HIM A *FAVOUR*. *NOTHING...* NEITHER *DAGGERS*, NOR *POISON*, NOR *REVOLUTION*, NOR *INVASION... NOTHING* CAN HARM HIM AGAIN!

COME ON, MY LORD, DON'T LOOK SO *DOWNCAST*. YOU MUST BE *BRIGHT AND HAPPY* AMONGST YOUR *GUESTS* TONIGHT.

SO I *WILL*, MY LOVE. AND SO, I HOPE, WILL *YOU*. I'D LIKE YOU TO PAY ATTENTION TO *BANQUO*. TREAT HIM AS A *SPECIAL GUEST... HUMOUR* HIM AND *FLATTER* HIM. WE'RE STILL NOT *SAFE* AND WE HAVE TO BE *PLEASANT* TO HIM FOR A WHILE *LONGER*. WE CAN'T ALLOW WHAT'S IN OUR *HEARTS* TO SHOW ON OUR *FACES*.

YOU MUST *STOP* THIS.

MY DEAR WIFE... MY MIND'S FULL OF *SCORPIONS!* YOU *KNOW* THAT *BANQUO* AND HIS SON *FLEANCE* ARE ALIVE...

THEY WON'T LIVE *FOREVER*.

MAYBE NOT! WE CAN TAKE COMFORT IN THE FACT THAT THEY'RE *VULNERABLE*. LISTEN, BEFORE THE *BAT* LEAVES HIS *CAVE* TONIGHT; BEFORE THE *WINGED BEETLE* ANSWERS THE *QUEEN OF HELL'S COMMAND* TO SIGNAL THE ARRIVAL OF *DARKNESS...* SOMETHING *SHOCKING* IS GOING TO BE DONE.

57

Act Three
Scene Three

Later, outside the King's Palace at Forres...

WHO TOLD *YOU* TO JOIN US?

MACBETH.

DOESN'T HE *TRUST* US? HE *TOLD* US WHAT TO DO, AND WE'RE GOING TO *DO* IT!

GET IN HERE *WITH* US, THEN! THERE'S STILL *LIGHT* IN THE SKY AND *LATE TRAVELLERS* ARE ON THE ROAD TRYING TO GET TO *SHELTER* FOR THE NIGHT. THE ONES WE'RE *WAITING* FOR WON'T BE LONG.

LISTEN! I HEAR HORSES.

Bring me a *light!*

IT MUST BE *HIM*. IT *CAN'T* BE ANYONE ELSE.

HIS *HORSES* HAVE GONE A *DIFFERENT WAY.*

BY ALMOST A *MILE.* HE'S DOING WHAT A *LOT* OF PEOPLE DO, *WALKING* THE REST OF THE WAY FROM HERE TO THE *PALACE GATE.*

THERE'S A LIGHT!

59

WHO PUT THE *LIGHT* OUT?

WASN'T THAT THE PLAN?

ONLY *ONE* OF 'EM IS DEAD. THE *SON'S* ESCAPED.

WE'VE ONLY DONE *HALF* THE JOB.

WELL, LET'S GO AND TELL HIM WHAT WE *HAVE* DONE.

Act Three
Scene Four

In the King's Palace, the banquet is about to commence...

YOU ALL KNOW YOUR OWN RANK. *COME IN* AND *SIT DOWN.* EVERYONE'S MOST WELCOME.

THANK YOU, YOUR MAJESTY.

I'LL BE A *HUMBLE HOST* AND TRY TO SPEND TIME WITH YOU *ALL.* OUR *HOSTESS* PREFERS TO KEEP HER *PLACE* FOR NOW, BUT SHE'LL WELCOME YOU ALL *LATER.*

GREET OUR FRIENDS FOR ME, SIR. MY *WELCOME* IS IN MY *HEART.*

SEE... THEY *RESPOND* BY THANKING YOU FROM THEIR *HEARTS.* SO *ALL IS WELL!* I'LL SIT HERE IN THE *MIDDLE* AND WE'LL HAVE A MOST *ENJOYABLE* TIME.

IN A *MOMENT,* WE SHALL ALL *DRINK* TOGETHER.

CLAP!!!

CLAP!!!

THUMP!!!

THUMP!!!

THERE'S *BLOOD* ON YOUR FACE.

IT'S *BANQUO'S.*

BETTER ON THE OUTSIDE OF *YOU* THAN ON THE *INSIDE* OF *HIM.* IS HE *DEAD?*

HIS *THROAT IS CUT,* MY LORD. I *KILLED* HIM.

THEN YOU'RE THE *BEST* OF CUT-THROATS. BUT WHOEVER DID THE SAME FOR *FLEANCE* IS EVEN *BETTER.* IF YOU DID *THAT,* YOU HAVE *NO EQUAL.*

MOST ROYAL SIR... *FLEANCE ESCAPED.*

THEN... HERE COME MY *DEMONS* AGAIN. JUST WHEN I WAS FEELING *GOOD;* AS STEADY AS *MARBLE,* SOLID AS A *ROCK,* FREE AS THE *AIR.* NOW, SUDDENLY... I FEEL *ENCLOSED, CRAMPED, CONFINED* AND *STIFLED* AGAIN BY *CREEPING DOUBTS* AND *FEARS.*

BUT *BANQUO'S DEAD?*

YES, MY GOOD LORD, DEAD AND BURIED IN A *DITCH,* WITH *TWENTY DEEP GASHES* IN HIS HEAD; *EACH ONE* OF THEM ENOUGH TO *KILL* HIM.

THANK YOU FOR THAT.

63

THE *ADULT* SNAKE IS *DEAD.* BUT THE *WORM* THAT'S *ESCAPED* WILL *MATURE* AND BECOME *VENOMOUS* IN TIME -- HE HAS *NO TEETH* AT THE MOMENT.

BE GONE FROM HERE. WE'LL TALK AGAIN *TOMORROW.*

MY ROYAL LORD, YOU'RE NEGLECTING YOUR *GUESTS.* WITHOUT OUR *HOSPITALITY,* THEY MIGHT AS WELL BE *PAYING* FOR THEIR MEAL AT AN *INN,* OR BE EATING AT *HOME.* IT'S THE *OCCASION* AND THE *CELEBRATION* THAT ADDS *FLAVOUR* TO THE MEAT. IT'S AN *EMPTY GATHERING* WITHOUT THAT.

THANK YOU FOR *REMINDING* ME.

TO YOUR *GOOD APPETITES* AND TO YOUR *VERY GOOD HEALTH!*

PLEASE *SIT DOWN,* YOUR *HIGHNESS.*

YOU CAN'T SAY *I* DID IT! DON'T GO SHAKING YOUR *BLOOD-SOAKED HAIR* AT ME!

STAND, GENTLEMEN. HIS MAJESTY IS *UNWELL.*

SIT! DEAR FRIENDS, MY LORD IS *OFTEN* LIKE THIS AND HAS BEEN SINCE *CHILDHOOD.* PLEASE, *KEEP* YOUR SEATS. IT'S ONLY A *BRIEF FIT;* HE'LL BE HIMSELF AGAIN IN A *MOMENT.* IT WILL *OFFEND* HIM AND MAKE HIM *WORSE* IF YOU TAKE TOO MUCH NOTICE. *EAT,* AND *IGNORE* HIM.

Are you a *man?*

Yes, and a *brave* one to look at something that would *frighten the devil.*

What *nonsense!* This is just a manifestation of your *fear.* The same thing as the *air-drawn dagger* that you said led you to *Duncan.* Come on, these outbursts are *ridiculous,* like some *old wive's tale* told around a *winter fire* by a *grandmother. Shame* on you!

WHY ARE YOU MAKING THESE *FACES?* WHEN ALL'S SAID AND DONE, YOU'RE ONLY LOOKING AT A *CHAIR.*

PLEASE, LOOK *THERE!* SEE! LOOK! *THERE!* WHAT DO YOU *SAY* NOW?

I *DON'T CARE!* IF YOU CAN *NOD,* YOU CAN *SPEAK* TOO. IF THE *DEAD* WON'T STAY IN THEIR *GRAVES* AND *TOMBS,* THEN WE SHOULD *FEED* THEM TO THE *BIRDS* OF *PREY.*

WHAT? HAS THIS *NONSENSE COMPLETELY DESTROYED* YOU?

AS *TRUE* AS I *STAND HERE...* I *SAW* HIM.

SHAME ON *YOU!*

BLOOD'S BEEN SPILLED *BEFORE* NOW. IN THE *OLDEN DAYS,* BEFORE WE BECAME *CIVILIZED...* AND *SINCE* THEN AS WELL. *TERRIBLE MURDERS* HAVE BEEN COMMITTED.

THERE *WAS* A TIME WHEN A MAN WOULD *DIE* WHEN HE HAD HIS *BRAINS KNOCKED OUT,* AND THAT'D BE THE *END* OF HIM...

IT'S *GONE*... AND I'M A *MAN* AGAIN.

PLEASE, *SIT DOWN.* You've *ruined the atmosphere* and *broken up the banquet* with your *insanity.*

CAN THESE THINGS *HAPPEN,* AS SUDDENLY AS A *SUMMER SHOWER...* AND YOU'RE NOT *AMAZED?* YOU'RE MAKING ME *DOUBT* MY *OWN SENSES,* IF YOU CAN SEE SUCH SIGHTS AND KEEP THE *COLOUR* IN YOUR CHEEKS, WHILE *MINE* ARE *BLEACHED WITH FEAR.*

PLEASE, *DON'T SPEAK* TO HIM. HE'S GETTING *WORSE AND WORSE.* QUESTIONS *INFURIATE* HIM. GOODNIGHT TO YOU ALL. DON'T WORRY ABOUT THE *ORDER OF LEAVING,* JUST *GO AT ONCE!*

GOODNIGHT. I HOPE HIS MAJESTY FEELS *BETTER* SOON.

WHAT SIGHTS, MY LORD?

GOODNIGHT TO YOU ALL!

IT WILL HAVE *BLOOD*, THEY SAY; *BLOOD* WILL HAVE *BLOOD!* STONES HAVE BEEN KNOWN TO *MOVE*, AND *TREES* TO *SPEAK.*

SORCERERS HAVE USED *MAGPIES*, CROWS AND *ROOKS* TO REVEAL *SECRET* MURDERS.

WHAT'S THE *TIME?*

IT'S ALMOST *MORNING.* DOES IT *MATTER?*

WHAT DO YOU THINK OF *MACDUFF'S* REFUSAL TO OBEY MY *COMMAND* AND ATTEND THE *BANQUET?*

DO YOU KNOW *WHY* HE DIDN'T COME?

I JUST HEARD *UNOFFICIALLY.* BUT I'LL FIND OUT FOR *SURE.* I HAVE *SPIES* IN *ALL THEIR* HOUSES.

TOMORROW I'LL GO AND FIND THE *WEIRD SISTERS.* I'LL GET THEM TO TELL ME *MORE.*

I'M *DETERMINED* TO KNOW THE *WORST,* BY ANY MEANS I CAN. I HAVE TO KNOW, FOR MY *OWN GOOD.* I'VE WADED *SO FAR* INTO THIS RIVER OF BLOOD, THAT *GOING BACK* NOW WOULD BE AS DIFFICULT AS TO *GO ON.* THERE ARE SOME THINGS THAT MUST BE DONE VERY SOON, BEFORE I *THINK* TOO MUCH ABOUT THEM.

YOU'RE BADLY IN NEED OF *SLEEP.*

COME, LET'S GO TO BED. THIS STRANGE *SELF-ABUSE* IS JUST A BEGINNER'S *STAGE-FRIGHT.* WE NEED TO GET *USED* TO THIS -- WE'RE *NEW* TO THIS KIND OF *KILLING.*

WITH THE HELP OF *GOD* AND *THESE TWO*, WE'LL SOON RESTORE *FOOD* TO OUR *TABLES* AND *SLEEP* TO OUR *NIGHTS*, PUTTING AN *END* TO THESE *MURDERS*. WE CAN SERVE OUR *RIGHTFUL KING* AND RECEIVE *HONEST REWARDS* FOR OUR LOYALTY -- ALL THOSE THINGS WE DON'T ENJOY *NOW*.

THIS NEWS FROM ENGLAND HAS *ENRAGED* MACBETH AND HE'S PREPARING HIS *DEFENCE* FOR AN *INVASION*.

DID HE SEND FOR *MACDUFF*?

HE *DID*. BUT WHEN HIS SURLY *MESSENGER* RETURNED WITH A *FLAT REFUSAL*, HE TURNED HIS *BACK* AND MUTTERED TO HIMSELF, AS IF TO SAY, "YOU'LL *REGRET* THAT ANSWER".

THAT OUGHT TO BE ENOUGH TO *WARN* MACDUFF TO BE *CAREFUL*. HE WOULD BE *WISE* TO *KEEP HIS DISTANCE*.

SOMEONE SHOULD GO TO THE *ENGLISH COURT* AND FIND OUT WHAT HIS *PLANS* ARE, BEFORE HE COMES BACK. *THAT* WAY, WE CAN BE *READY* TO HELP BRING THE *BLESSING OF PEACE* BACK TO OUR SUFFERING COUNTRY!

WHOEVER GOES, I'LL SEND MY *PRAYERS* WITH HIM.

79

POUR IN SOW'S BLOOD, THAT HAS EATEN HER OWN PIGLETS; GREASE, THAT'S SWEATEN FROM THE MURDERER'S GIBBET, THROW INTO THE FLAME.

COME, HIGH OR LOW; YOURSELF AND STATUS, QUICKLY SHOW!

TELL ME, YOU UNKNOWN POWER...

HE KNOWS YOUR THOUGHT: HEAR HIS SPEECH, BUT SAY YOU NOUGHT.

MACBETH! MACBETH! MACBETH! BEWARE MACDUFF; BEWARE THE THANE OF FIFE. DISMISS ME. ENOUGH.

WHATEVER YOU ARE, THANK YOU FOR THE WARNING. YOU'VE GUESSED MY FEAR. BUT ONE MORE WORD...

HE WILL NOT BE COMMANDED. HERE'S ANOTHER, MORE POWERFUL THAN THE FIRST.

MACBETH! MACBETH! MACBETH!

IF I HAD THREE EARS, I'D HEAR YOU.

BE BLOODY, BOLD AND RESOLUTE: LAUGH TO SCORN THE POWER OF MAN, FOR NONE OF WOMAN BORN SHALL HARM MACBETH.

THEN LIVE, MACDUFF! I DON'T NEED TO BE AFRAID OF YOU. BUT... BETTER TO BE ABSOLUTELY CERTAIN. I'LL MAKE SURE YOU DON'T LIVE. THAT WAY, I WON'T NEED TO WORRY ABOUT YOU AND I CAN SLEEP SOUNDLY AT NIGHT.

WHAT'S THIS RISING UP... IT LOOKS LIKE A PRINCE, WEARING A CROWN ON HIS YOUNG HEAD?

LISTEN, BUT DO NOT SPEAK TO IT.

85

89

THERE'S NO *DEVIL* AMONGST THE *LEGIONS OF HELL* MORE EVIL THAN *MACBETH.*

A LACK OF SELF-DISCIPLINE IS A *BAD* FAULT. IT'S BROUGHT DOWN *MANY* A KING. BUT DON'T BE AFRAID TO *TAKE BACK* WHAT'S *YOURS.*

YOU COULD HAVE AS *MUCH PLEASURE* AS YOU *WANT* IN *PRIVATE* AND STILL SEEM *PRINCIPLED* IN *PUBLIC.* WE'VE ENOUGH *WILLING DAMES.* YOU CAN'T BE SO *INSATIABLE* THAT YOU'D GET THROUGH *ALL THE WOMEN* WHO'D BE PREPARED TO GIVE THEMSELVES TO A *KING?*

I *GRANT* YOU, HE'S *BLOODY* AND *BLATANT, GREEDY* AND *LYING, DECEITFUL, AGGRESSIVE, MALICIOUS* AND FULL OF EVERY *SIN* IN THE BOOK; *BUT* THERE'S NO *END* TO MY *LUST. NONE!*

YOUR *WIVES,* YOUR *DAUGHTERS,* YOUR *MOTHERS* AND YOUR *MAIDS,* COULDN'T SATISFY MY *LUST* AND *DESIRE.* I'D ALLOW *NOTHING* TO GET IN MY WAY. NO, IT'S BETTER THAT *MACBETH* SHOULD RULE.

MAYBE, BUT I'M ALSO SO *GREEDY* THAT, IF I WERE KING, I'D TAKE *ALL THE NOBLES' LANDS.*

I'D WANT THIS ONE'S *JEWELS* AND THAT ONE'S *HOUSE* AND, THE MORE I *HAD,* THE MORE I'D *WANT.* I'D EVEN START *FIGHTS* WITH GOOD AND LOYAL SUBJECTS TO *DESTROY* THEM FOR THEIR *WEALTH.*

THIS *GREED* IS *BAD.* IT'S *WORSE* THAN LUST. AND IT'S BROUGHT MANY OF OUR KINGS TO *GRIEF.* STILL, DON'T WORRY; THE CROWN OF SCOTLAND HAS ENOUGH WEALTH TO *SATISFY* YOU, WITHOUT HAVING TO TAKE FROM *OTHERS.* THESE VICES ARE *ACCEPTABLE,* WHEN WEIGHED AGAINST YOUR *VIRTUES.*

MACDUFF! YOUR *HONEST REACTION* HAS *REMOVED* MY SUSPICION AND CONVINCED ME OF YOUR *LOYALTY.*

THAT *DEVIL MACBETH* HAS TRIED TO *TRICK* ME *SEVERAL* TIMES AND IT'S MADE ME *CAUTIOUS.* BUT *GOD ABOVE* HAS BROUGHT US TOGETHER AND I'LL AGREE TO BE *GUIDED* BY YOU.

I *WITHDRAW* ALL THE THINGS I SAID ABOUT MYSELF. THAT'S *NOT* HOW I AM.

I'VE NEVER EVEN *BEEN* WITH A *WOMAN;* NEVER *PERJURED* MYSELF; HARDLY EVER *COVETED* WHAT WASN'T *MINE;* NEVER *BROKE MY PROMISE;* WOULDN'T *BETRAY* EVEN *ONE DEVIL* TO *ANOTHER* AND I LOVE THE *TRUTH* AS MUCH AS *LIFE IT SELF.*

THIS IS THE FIRST TIME I'VE EVER *LIED.*

MY *TRUE SELF* IS *YOURS* AND MY *COUNTRY'S* TO *COMMAND.* BEFORE YOU CAME, OLD *SIWARD* WAS READY TO MARCH WITH TEN THOUSAND GOOD SOLDIERS. NOW WE'LL GO *TOGETHER* AND *VICTORY* WILL BE THE RESULT OF OUR ARGUMENT!

WHY DON'T YOU *SAY* SOMETHING?

YOU HAD ME *CONFUSED* FOR A WHILE. IT'S HARD TO *RECONCILE* THE THINGS YOU'VE JUST SAID.

WAIT A MOMENT.

An English doctor approaches...

WILL THE *KING* BE COMING OUT?

YES, SIR. THERE'S A *QUEUE* OF *SICK PEOPLE* WAITING FOR HIM TO *CURE* THEM. THEIR DISEASE *DEFEATS* OUR *MEDICINE,* BUT *GOD* HAS GIVEN SUCH *HEALING POWERS* TO HIS TOUCH, THAT THEY'RE *CURED IMMEDIATELY.*

THANK YOU, DOCTOR.

99

POOR COUNTRY! IT'S ALMOST *AFRAID* OF ITSELF. IT CAN'T BE CALLED OUR *MOTHER* ANY MORE, JUST OUR *GRAVE*. IT'S A PLACE WHERE ONLY THE *STUPID* SMILE;

WHERE NOBODY TAKES ANY *NOTICE* OF THE *SIGHS* AND *GROANS* AND *SHRIEKS* THAT CAN BE HEARD EVERYWHERE, AND WHERE *VIOLENCE* AND *SORROW* ARE *COMMONPLACE*. NOBODY ASKS WHO THE *FUNERAL BELL* TOLLS FOR ANY MORE AND *GOOD MEN'S LIVES* ARE SHORTER THAN THE LIVES OF THE *FLOWERS* THEY WEAR IN THEIR *HATS*.

I KNOW IT'S *TRUE*, COUSIN!

WHAT'S THE *LATEST* TRAGEDY?

IF IT'S AN *HOUR OLD*, IT'S ALREADY *STALE*. THERE'S A *NEW* ONE EVERY *MINUTE*.

HOW IS MY *WIFE*?

WHY... SHE'S *WELL*.

AND MY *CHILDREN*?

WELL TOO.

THE TYRANT HASN'T *BOTHERED* THEM?

NO, THEY WERE *FINE*... WHEN I *LEFT* THEM.

YOU'RE HOLDING SOMETHING *BACK*. WHAT *IS* IT?

101

Late at night in
Dunsinane Castle...

WE'VE BEEN *WATCHING* FOR *TWO NIGHTS* AND I'M BEGINNING TO *DOUBT* YOUR *STORY*. WHEN DID YOU SAY SHE LAST WALKED?

SINCE HIS *MAJESTY* WENT TO *WAR*, I'VE SEEN HER GET OUT OF BED AND PUT ON HER NIGHTGOWN, THEN UNLOCK HER *CABINET*, TAKE OUT PAPER, *FOLD* IT, *WRITE* ON IT, *READ* IT, THEN *SEAL* IT AND GO BACK TO *BED* AGAIN. AND ALL THE TIME SHE'S *FAST ASLEEP*.

IT'S QUITE *UNNATURAL* FOR HER TO BE *ASLEEP* AND BEHAVE AS IF SHE'S *AWAKE* AT THE *SAME TIME*. BESIDES *WALKING* AND THE *OTHER* THINGS, HAVE YOU HEARD HER *SAY* ANYTHING WHILE SHE'S IN THIS STATE?

I WON'T *REPEAT* IT, SIR.

YOU CAN TELL *ME*. IT'S ONLY *RIGHT* THAT YOU DO.

NOT TO *YOU*, NOR *ANYONE*. I HAVE NO *WITNESS* TO *BACK ME UP*.

LOOK, HERE SHE *COMES*. THIS IS *EXACTLY* HOW IT WAS *BEFORE*...

...and there, you see, she's *fast asleep*. *Watch* her, but don't *move*.

Where did she get that *light?*

it was by her *bedside.* She has a light with her at *all times.* She *ordered* it.

You see, her *eyes* are *open.*

Yes, but there's no *sense* in them.

What's she doing *now?* Look how she's *rubbing her hands.*

She *always* does that, as if she's *washing* them. I've known her to do it for a *quarter of an hour.*

THERE'S STILL A *STAIN.*

Listen! She's speaking. I'll *write down* what she says so that I can *remember* it.

OUT, DAMNED SPOT! *OUT,* I SAY!

ONE, TWO: WHY THEN, IT'S TIME TO *DO* IT.

HELL'S DARK!

SHAME, MY LORD, SHAME! A *SOLDIER* AND *AFRAID?*

WHY SHOULD WE *CARE* WHO KNOWS? *NO-ONE* CAN QUESTION OUR *POWER.*

BUT WHO'D HAVE THOUGHT THE OLD MAN HAD SO MUCH *BLOOD* IN HIM?

105

WASH YOUR HANDS AND PUT ON YOUR NIGHTGOWN. DON'T LOOK SO PALE.

I'LL TELL YOU AGAIN, BANQUO'S BURIED, HE CAN'T COME OUT OF HIS GRAVE.

That too?

TO BED, TO BED. THERE'S SOMEONE KNOCKING AT THE GATE. COME, COME, COME, COME... GIVE ME YOUR HAND. WHAT'S DONE CANNOT BE UNDONE.

TO BED, TO BED, TO BED.

WILL SHE GO BACK TO BED NOW?

STRAIGHT AWAY.

THERE ARE TERRIBLE RUMOURS GOING AROUND. HEARTLESS CRIMES CAN CREATE MADNESS LIKE THIS AND SICK MINDS TELL THEIR SECRETS TO THEIR PILLOWS. SHE HAS MORE NEED OF A PRIEST THAN A PHYSICIAN.

GOD FORGIVE US ALL!

LOOK AFTER HER. REMOVE ANYTHING SHE COULD USE TO HARM HERSELF. AND DON'T TAKE YOUR EYES OFF HER.

GOODNIGHT. SHE HAS BAFFLED MY MIND AND SURPRISED MY EYES. I CAN THINK, BUT I DARE NOT SPEAK.

GOODNIGHT, DOCTOR.

107

Act Five
Scene Two

The Scottish countryside, near Dunsinane...

THE **ENGLISH FORCES** ARE **CLOSE**, LED BY **MALCOLM**, HIS UNCLE **SIWARD** AND THE GOOD **MACDUFF**. THEY WANT **REVENGE**, AND EVEN A **DEAD** MAN WOULD SEE THE **JUSTICE** OF THEIR CAUSE.

WE'LL MEET THEM NEAR **BIRNAM WOOD** – THEY'RE TRAVELLING THAT WAY.

DOES ANYONE KNOW IF **DONALBAIN** IS WITH HIS BROTHER?

I KNOW FOR CERTAIN HE'S **NOT**, SIR. I HAVE A **LIST** OF ALL THE **OFFICERS.** SIWARD'S **SON** IS ON IT AND MANY **OTHER** YOUNG MEN IN THEIR FIRST FLUSH OF MANHOOD.

WHAT'S THE **TYRANT** UP TO?

HE'S **DEFENDING** HIMSELF AT **DUNSINANE**. SOME SAY HE'S GONE **MAD;** OTHERS, WHO DON'T **HATE** HIM SO MUCH, CALL IT **COURAGEOUS ANGER.** BUT **ONE** THING'S FOR SURE, HE **NO** LONGER CONTROLS OUR **COUNTRY.**

HIS **SECRET MURDERS** ARE COMING BACK TO **HAUNT** HIM NOW AND HIS MEN **DESERT** HIM BY THE **MINUTE.** THOSE STILL **WITH** HIM DON'T HAVE THEIR **HEARTS** IN IT.

HIS **TITLE** IS HANGING **LOOSELY** AROUND HIM, LIKE A **GIANT'S ROBE** ON A **PETTY THIEF.**

WHY DON'T YOU *SLASH YOUR FACE* AND COVER UP YOUR *PALENESS* WITH *BLOOD*, YOU LILY-LIVERED BOY. *WHAT* SOLDIERS, CLOWN? *DAMN YOU*, YOUR *WHITE CHEEKS* SMELL OF *FEAR*. *WHAT SOLDIERS, PALE-FACE?*

THE *ENGLISH FORCE...* IF YOU PLEASE.

GET YOUR FACE OUT OF HERE!

SEYTON!

IT MAKES ME *SICK* TO SEE...

SEYTON!

THIS *INVASION* WILL SETTLE MATTERS *ONE WAY* OR THE *OTHER.* I'VE *LIVED* LONG ENOUGH. MY *AMBITION* HAS TURNED INTO A *DRY, WITHERED LEAF.*

ALL THE THINGS THAT SHOULD BE ENJOYED IN OLD AGE... *HONOUR, LOVE, RESPECT* AND *FRIENDS*, I WON'T HAVE *ANY* OF THEM. INSTEAD, PEOPLE WILL *CURSE* ME... MAYBE NOT *OUT LOUD*, BUT FROM *DEEP INSIDE THEIR HEARTS.*

111

113

HAVE YOU LOST YOUR *TONGUE?* SPEAK UP... *QUICKLY!*

MY GRACIOUS LORD, I *WANT* TO REPORT WHAT I THOUGHT I SAW, BUT I DON'T KNOW HOW TO *DO* IT.

WELL, JUST SAY IT!

WHILE I WAS STANDING WATCH ON THE HILL, I LOOKED TOWARD *BIRNAM* AND, SUDDENLY, I THOUGHT THE *WOOD* BEGAN TO *MOVE.*

LIAR! PEASANT!

I *DESERVE* YOUR ANGER IF I'M *WRONG.* BUT YOU CAN SEE IT COMING LESS THAN *THREE MILES* AWAY... I'M TELLING YOU, A *MOVING WOOD.*

IF YOU'RE *LYING,* YOU'LL *HANG* FROM THE *NEAREST TREE* UNTIL YOU *STARVE.* IF YOU'RE TELLING THE *TRUTH,* THEN I *DON'T CARE* IF THE SAME THING HAPPENS TO *ME.*

I MUST BE *STRONG* AND *QUESTION* THE DOUBLETALK OF THE *HELL-HAGS* WHO LIED WITH STRAIGHT FACES WHEN THEY SAID "DON'T BE AFRAID, 'TIL BIRNAM WOOD COMES TO DUNSINANE". *AND NOW A WOOD COMES TOWARD DUNSINANE.*

ARM YOURSELVES AND GET OUT ONTO THE BATTLEFIELD!

IF WHAT HE SAYS IS *TRUE,* THERE'S *NOWHERE TO HIDE.* I'M *TIRED* OF LOOKING AT THE SUN AND I WISH... I WISH THE *WORLD* WAS NOW *OVER* AND *DONE.*

RING THE *ALARM!* I'M READY TO *ATTACK!* AT LEAST WE'LL DIE WITH ARMOUR ON OUR BACK!

119

YOU WERE *BORN OF A WOMAN.* AND I *SMILE* AT *SWORDS* AND *LAUGH* AT WEAPONS WIELDED BY *ANY* MAN WHO WAS BORN OF A WOMAN.

THERE'S *NOISE* OVER THERE.

SHOW YOUR FACE, TYRANT! IF *ANYONE ELSE* KILLS YOU, I'LL BE HAUNTED BY THE GHOSTS OF MY WIFE AND CHILDREN *FOREVER!*

I CAN'T KILL *POOR SOLDIERS* WHO'VE BEEN *FORCED INTO* THIS FIGHT.

I *WANT* YOU, *MACBETH!* OR I'LL PUT MY *SWORD* BACK IN ITS SCABBARD *UNUSED.*

123

125

I WISH OUR *MISSING FRIENDS* WERE HERE.

SOME HAD TO DIE. BUT, WHEN I LOOK AROUND, I SEE THIS *GREAT VICTORY* HAS BEEN WON WITHOUT TOO MANY *CASUALTIES*.

MACDUFF IS MISSING, AND SO IS YOUR NOBLE *SON*.

YOUR *SON* HAS PAID A *SOLDIER'S PRICE*, MY LORD. HE WAS SCARCELY A *MAN*, BUT WITH *SKILL* AND *RESOLVE* HE *FOUGHT* AND *DIED* LIKE ONE.

THEN... HE'S *DEAD?*

YES, AND CARRIED OFF THE FIELD. YOUR *SORROW* MUSTN'T BE MEASURED BY HIS *WORTH*, BECAUSE IT WOULD HAVE NO *END*.

WERE HIS *WOUNDS* ON THE *FRONT* OF HIS *BODY?*

YES, ON THE FRONT.

WELL THEN, HE'S *GOD'S* SOLDIER! IF I HAD AS MANY *SONS* AS I HAVE *HAIRS,* I COULDN'T *WISH* THEM A BETTER DEATH. HIS *TIME* HAD COME.

NO, HE *DOESN'T.* THEY SAY HE DIED *BRAVELY* AND DID HIS *DUTY.* AND SO, *GOD BE WITH HIM!*

HE DESERVES *MORE GRIEVING* THAN THAT, AND HE'LL *GET* IT.

LOOK, HERE COMES *BETTER* NEWS.

HAIL, *KING!* FOR THAT'S WHAT YOU *ARE.* HERE'S THE *USURPER'S CURSED HEAD. FREEDOM* AT LAST! I SEE YOU SURROUNDED BY YOUR KINGDOM'S *FINEST,* ALL THINKING THE WORDS I WANT THEM TO *SHOUT OUT NOW:*

HAIL, KING OF SCOTLAND!

HAIL, KING OF SCOTLAND!

NG!!!

BANG!!!

BANG!!!

WE'LL *SWIFTLY REWARD* EVERY *ONE* OF YOU. MY *THANES* AND *KINSMEN,* FROM *NOW ON* YOU ARE *EARLS* - THE *FIRST* IN SCOTLAND TO *HAVE* THAT TITLE.

WE MUST ALSO *BRING HOME,* WITHOUT DELAY, OUR *FRIENDS* WHO WENT INTO *EXILE* TO ESCAPE THE ASSASSINATIONS OF THIS *DEAD BUTCHER* AND HIS *FIENDISH QUEEN* WHO, WE HEAR, *KILLED HERSELF.*

127

William Shakespeare

(c.1564 - 1616 AD)

William Shakespeare is one of the most widely read authors and possibly the best dramatist ever to live. The actual date of his birth is not known, but traditionally April 23rd 1564 (St George's Day) has been his accepted birthday, as this was three days before his baptism. He died on the same date in 1616, aged fifty-two.

The life of William Shakespeare can be divided into three acts. The first twenty years of his life were spent in Stratford-upon-Avon where he grew up, went to school, got married and became a father. The next twenty-five years he spent as an actor and playwright in London; and he spent his last few years back in Stratford-upon-Avon, where he enjoyed his retirement in moderate wealth gained from his successful years in the theatre.

William was the eldest son of tradesman John Shakespeare and Mary Arden, and the third of eight children. His father was later elected mayor of Stratford, which was the highest post a man in civic politics could attain. In sixteenth-century England, William was lucky to survive into adulthood; syphilis, scurvy, smallpox, tuberculosis, typhus and dysentery shortened life expectancy at the time to approximately thirty-five years. The Bubonic Plague took the lives of many and was believed to have been the cause of death for three of William's seven siblings.

Little is known of William's childhood, other than it is thought that he attended the local grammar school, where he studied Latin and English Literature. In 1582, at the age of eighteen, William married a local farmer's daughter, Anne Hathaway, who was eight years his senior and three months pregnant. During their marriage they had three children: Susanna, born on May 26th 1583 and twins, Hamnet and Judith, born on February 2nd 1585. Hamnet, William's only son, caught Bubonic Plague and died aged just eleven.

Five years into his marriage William moved to London and appeared in many small parts at The Globe Theatre, then one of the biggest theatres in England. His first appearance in public as a poet was in 1593 with "Venus and Adonis" and again in the following year with "The Rape of Lucrece". Six years later, in 1599, he became joint proprietor of The Globe Theatre.

When Queen Elizabeth died in 1603, she was succeeded by her cousin King James of Scotland. King James supported Shakespeare and his band of actors and gave them license to call themselves "The King's Men" in return for entertaining the court.

In just twenty-three years, between 1590 and 1613, William Shakespeare is attributed with writing thirty-eight plays, one-hundred-and-fifty-four sonnets and five poems. No original manuscript exists for any of his plays, so it is hard to accurately date them. However, from their contents and reports of the day it is believed that his first play was "The Taming of the Shrew" and that his last complete work was "Two Noble Kinsmen", written two years before he died. The cause of his death remains unknown.

He was buried on April 25th 1616, two days after his death, at the Church of the Holy Trinity (the same Church where he had been baptised fifty-two years earlier). His gravestone bears these words, believed to have been written by William himself:-

"Good friend for Jesus sake forbear,
To dig the dust enclosed here!
Blest be the man that spares these stones,
And curst be he that moves my bones"

At the time of his death, William had substantial properties, which he bestowed on his family and associates from the theatre.

In his will he left his wife, the former Anne Hathaway, his second best bed!

William Shakespeare's last direct descendant died in 1670. She was his granddaughter, Elizabeth.

The Real Macbeth

(c.1005 - 1057 AD)

Macbeth is one of Shakespeare's most famous characters. It is a name that's known the whole world over; but many people don't realise that the story is linked to actual historical events — even though those events have been heavily embellished and altered for the sake of entertainment.

Shakespeare obtained his information about the real Macbeth from Raphael Holinshed's book, "The Chronicles of England, Scotland and Ireland", published in 1574 (which Shakespeare used as a primary resource for all of his historical plays). Holinshed himself derived his information from a variety of sources, most notably Andrew of Wyntoun's "Orygynale Cronykil" ("Original Chronicle") which traces a history of Scotland from Biblical times, and Hector Boece's

"Scotorum Historiae" ("Scottish History"), published in 1526 and translated from Latin into English by John Bellenden in 1535.

Macbeth, or rather Mac Bethad as he would have been called, was King of Scotland from 1040 to 1057 (although in Shakespeare's play, his reign is made to appear significantly less than seventeen years). The name "Mac Bethad" means

"son of life", and is actually Irish, rather than Scottish in origin.

Eleventh century Scotland was a barbaric land; with war and ruthless slaughter being a fact of life. Survival depended on having a strong and capable local ruler or chieftain to protect both life and property. Such a leader would provide a strong paternalistic rule, guarding the family, community and land from all enemies.

Some of these enemies could be, and often were, collections of distant family members challenging the current leadership.

A number of local rulers would often unite under the nominal leadership of one 'king' to promote their common interests and to wage war on other more distant clans. Interestingly, in those times, kings and rulers could name their own successor — it wasn't a privilege that was handed down from parent to eldest child as the monarchy operates today. However, family linkage tended to be respected and the title usually passed to a relative of the king — selected as being the one most suitable for immediate rule, and not necessarily the natural heir. Understandably, this selection process would have been challenged, especially by those individuals who felt that they had a greater right to become king than the person taking on the title. Such grievances were often dealt with or pre-empted by the murdering of family members judged unsuitable for power, to ensure that the 'favourite' won the race.

Macbeth was the son of Findláech mac Ruaidrí (who was a High Steward of Moray) in the north of Scotland, around 1005. His mother's name is unknown, and indeed her own parentage is inaccurately recorded. It is uncertain whether she was the daughter of King

Kenneth II or of King Malcolm II. However, that is largely immaterial as whichever man was Macbeth's grandfather, would be a strong enough family link for him to make a claim for the throne.

In 1020, Macbeth's father Findláech died. It is thought that he was killed, most probably by his brother Máel Brigté's son Máel Coluim (Malcolm). Findláech's title of High Steward went to his nephew Gille Coemgáin. In 1032, Gille Coemgáin and fifty other people were burned to death as punishment for the murder of Findláech. This act of retribution could well have been carried out by

Macbeth and his allies. Following Gille Coemgáin's death, Macbeth took the title of High Steward of Moray.

It was around this time that he married Gille Coemgáin's widow, Gruoch, and became step-father to her son, Lulach (which explains why Shakespeare has Lady Macbeth talk about motherhood, whereas at no time does Macbeth make any reference to being a father. Moreover, Macduff states that Macbeth has no children in Act IV Scene III (page 102)). Macbeth's marriage to Gruoch was significant, because she was the grand-daughter of Kenneth III. Therefore through their combined

ancestors the marriage ensured that Macbeth had a strong claim to the throne.

Within a very short space of time, Macbeth's rival Gille Coemgáin had not only lost his life, but his title and his widowed wife had gone swiftly to Macbeth.

While Macbeth was a high-ranking lord of Moray, the King at the time was Donnchad mac Crináin (King Duncan I). Duncan succeeded to the throne when his grandfather, King Malcolm II died at Glamis. It is thought likely that Malcolm had engineered the position of Duncan taking over from him, through the tactical assassination of any family members who might feel they had a stronger claim to the crown.

Given the circumstances, it would have been a sensible course of action for Duncan to make peace with his remaining family, in particular his cousin Thorfinn the Mighty (Earl of Orkney), his cousin Macbeth, and the person closest to his throne in terms of lineage, namely Gruoch, the wife of Macbeth. Duncan appears to have been unsuccessful in uniting the "royal family", and Macbeth pressed his own claim to the throne with the help of that same cousin and ally, Earl Thorfinn of Orkney. He eventually won the crown by slaying Duncan at Bothgowanan near Elgin in 1040.

Macbeth has been judged by history to be a more able king than his predecessor. Under his rule the kingdom became relatively stable and reasonably prosperous, so much so, that by 1050 he was confident enough to leave the country for a number of months and make a pilgrimage to Rome. At this time he was said to have been so wealthy that he "scattered alms like seed corn". As Wyntoun's "Orygynale Cronykil" says:-

"In pilgrimage þidder he come,
And in almus he sew siluer"

All was not peaceful, however, and in 1054 Duncan I's son, Máel Coluim mac Donnchada (Malcolm Canmore, nicknamed 'big head'), challenged Macbeth for the throne of Scotland. He did so in alliance with Siward, Earl of Northumbria (who also happened to be the cousin of Duncan's widow) and they took control of much of southern Scotland. Three years later, on 15 August 1057 Macbeth's army was finally defeated at the Battle of Lumphanan, in Aberdeenshire. Macbeth was killed in battle. He is believed to be buried in the graveyard at Saint Oran's Chapel on the Isle of Iona, the last of many Kings of Alba and Dalriada to be laid to rest there. This site is also supposed to be the final resting place of King Duncan I.

Unlike in Shakespeare's play, the killing of Macbeth didn't result in the crown going straight to Duncan's son Malcolm. It first went to Macbeth's step-son Lulach, on the basis that Kenneth III was his maternal great-grandfather. Lulach was a weak king and ridiculed, being called "Lulach the Simple" or "Lulach the Fool". After a few months of rule, he was murdered; and Malcolm, son of Duncan I, became King Malcolm III of Scotland.

No-one knows what happened to Lady Macbeth. Dramatically, Shakespeare has her losing her sanity and taking her own life – however there is no record of that happening, or even of her falling to a bloody death. Having lived through the murder of her first husband, the killing of her second husband in battle, and the murder of her son, even if she was to outlive them all, it's unlikely that she enjoyed any form of happiness.

Macbeth and the Kings of Scotland

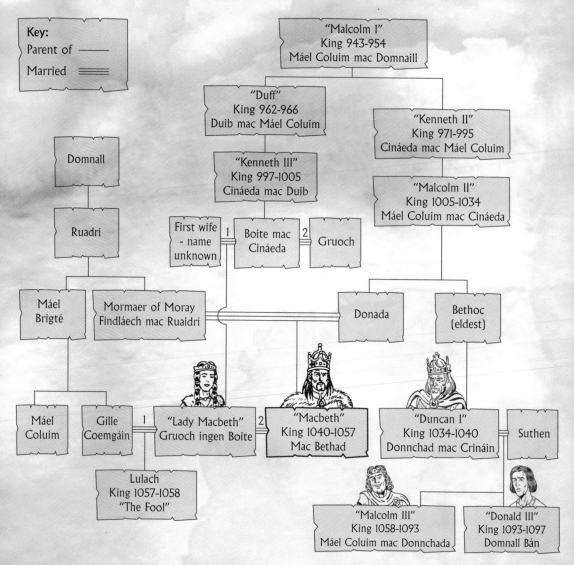

Key:
Parent of ——————
Married ══════

"Malcolm I"
King 943-954
Máel Coluim mac Domnaill

"Duff"
King 962-966
Duib mac Máel Coluim

"Kenneth II"
King 971-995
Cináeda mac Máel Coluim

Domnall

"Kenneth III"
King 997-1005
Cináeda mac Duib

"Malcolm II"
King 1005-1034
Máel Coluim mac Cináeda

Ruadri

First wife - name unknown | 1 | Boite mac Cináeda | 2 | Gruoch

Máel Brigté

Mormaer of Moray
Findláech mac Ruaidrí

Donada

Bethoc (eldest)

Máel Coluim

Gille Coemgáin | 1 | "Lady Macbeth" Gruoch ingen Boite | 2 | "Macbeth" King 1040-1057 Mac Bethad

"Duncan I"
King 1034-1040
Donnchad mac Crináin

Suthen

Lulach
King 1057-1058
"The Fool"

"Malcolm III"
King 1058-1093
Máel Coluim mac Donnchada

"Donald III"
King 1093-1097
Domnall Bán

The Macbeth Murder Trail

1020 – Macbeth's father Findláech died – thought to have been killed by his own nephew, Máel Coluim. His title of High Steward went to Máel Coluim's brother, Gille Coemgáin.

1032 – Gille Coemgáin and 50 other people were burned to death as punishment for the killing of Findláech. Thought to have been carried out by Macbeth and his allies as retribution for killing his father. Macbeth takes his title (that had been his father's) and also takes Gille Coemgáin's widow, Gruoch, for his wife.

There is another theory, that Gille Coemgáin killed Boite mac Cináeda because he had made his wife the heiress to his estate. As retaliation for this murder, Boite's wife

Gruoch (the stepmother of the Gruoch that married Gille Coemgáin and later Macbeth) mustered an army to kill Gille Coemgáin.

1040 – Macbeth killed King Duncan I at Bothgowanan.

1050 – Macbeth went on a pilgrimage to Rome.

1054 – Máel Coluim mac Donnchada (Malcolm, son of King Duncan I) stakes his claim to the throne and challenges Macbeth in the first of a series of battles.

1057 – Macbeth's army is finally defeated by Malcolm's army at the Battle of Lumphanan. Macbeth is killed in battle. Macbeth's step-son Lulach becomes King.

1057 – After only a few months of rule, Malcolm kills Lulach and becomes King Malcolm III of Scotland.

The History of Shakespeare's Macbeth

When comparing the play to the actual historical events, it is clear that those events were merely inspiration for Shakespeare's own take on the story. It is unlikely that he deliberately intended to misrepresent the facts; however it is important to recognise that as a playwright, Shakespeare had a responsibility to entertain his audience with his works. Therefore, what takes place on the stage is an artistic modification of what took place in history; to give the best portrayal of the plots and motives of the characters in order to arrive at a worthy spectacle. Amongst other things, Shakespeare possessed good business sense — and a successful play would draw in the fee-paying public to provide him and his troupe with an income.

But money was not his sole concern. His position in society was paramount, and of prime importance was the need to pander to the monarch.

Macbeth is thought to have been written to be performed in honour of a royal visit by the King of Denmark to King James I in 1606. King James I became King of England in 1603 when Elizabeth I died. He was already King of Scotland (King James VI of Scotland). Interestingly, James I was a keen scholar, and had a deep interest in witchcraft; so much so that he wrote a book on the subject which he called

"Daemonologie", in 1597, and in it he advocated that witches should be dealt with severely. In addition, he was a keen supporter of the arts, having the title of "The King's Men" bestowed upon Shakespeare's acting company soon after his coronation. In return, The King's Men were expected to perform at court whenever they were asked, which amounted to around a dozen performances each year.

Setting the play in Scotland and including elements of witchcraft appears to be a deliberate attempt by Shakespeare to please the new King. But he can't take the credit for including witchcraft in the tale of Macbeth: we have Holinshed to thank for that. Raphael Holinshed's "Chronicles of England, Scotland and Ireland", first published in 1574, was a primary source of reference for a number of Shakespeare's plays, and Macbeth is no exception. The following extract from Holinshed's Chronicles demonstrates just how closely Shakespeare borrowed from his version of events:

"It fortuned as Makbeth and Banquho iournied towards Fores, where the king then laie, they went sporting by the waie together without other company saue onelie themselues, passing thorough the woods and fields, when suddenlie in the middest of a laund, there met them three women in strange and wild apparell, resembling creatures of the elder world, whome when they attentiuelie beheld, woondering much at the sight, the first of them spake and said: All haile Makbeth, thane of Glammis (for he had latelie entered into that dignitie and office by the death of his father Sinell). The second of them said: Haile Makbeth thane of Cawder. But the third said: All haile Makbeth that heereafter shalt be king of Scotland.

Then Banquho: What manner of women (saith he) are you, that seeme so little fauourable vnto me, whereas to my fellow heere, besides high offices, ye assigne also the kingdome, appointing foorth nothing for me at all? Yes, (saith the first of them) we promise greater benefits vnto thee, than vnto him, for he shall reigne in deed, but with an vnluckie end: neither shall he leaue anie issue behind him to succeed in his place, where contrarilie thou in deed shalt not reigne at all, but of thee those shall be borne which shall gouern the Scotish kingdome by long order of continuall descent. Herewith the foresaid women vanished immediatlie out of their sight."

In those days, the Stuart Kings of Scotland (King James I was a Stuart) were believed to have descended from Banquo (this is unproven but may have some truth in it). The witches "predicted" a long line of kings and this is dealt with in the play verbally in Act I Scene III (page 15), and visually in Act IV Scene I (page 85) when Macbeth is shown a large number of kings in a line, that all bear a resemblance to Banquo. The "bloodline" is only made possible by Fleance escaping when his father is attacked. Holinshed describes how Walter Steward, the founder of the Stuart royal family, who married the daughter of Robert Bruce was a descendent of Fleance and therefore Banquo. This ancestral connection must have been behind a change that Shakespeare made to Holinshed's accounts, namely that in Holinshed, Banquo was an accomplice in Duncan's murder; to show an ancestor of the King to have acted unlawfully would have

been rather foolhardy on Shakespeare's part. Other pandering includes the reference to the English King (Edward the Confessor) having God-given powers to cure "the evil" in Act IV Scene III (page 99), also known as Scrofula. Edward was believed to have that power, and King James I revived the custom of sufferers being "touched" by the monarch as a cure for it.

But it is with his portrayal of the witches where Shakespeare really aimed to please the King. In his book, King James denounced witchcraft absolutely. It was his belief that witches were mostly women who had masculine features, typified by facial hair. They were in league with the devil, could summon up spirits, and could even curse images of people to control their destiny. These were early days in the understanding of witchcraft, and the very subject was a threat to King James' belief of divine right of kingship. In his world,

witchcraft was a devil-based display of evil that was an ever-present challenge to the sanctity of his God-given ruling. It is a general fear of witchcraft, then, that is the possible reason why neither Holinshed nor Shakespeare ever refer to the women as witches. In fact, the elements of witchcraft that exist in the play, particularly the spells and the appearance of Hecate, are now believed to be later additions, made by Thomas Middleton following on from his own play, "The Witch". The term only appears once, in Act I Scene III (page 12*) and even then it could be an insult being reported by the speaker.

Beyond the belief that it was written for the visit of the King of Denmark in 1606, a number of other elements point towards it being authored in that year. The Porter's ramblings in Act II Scene III (page 38*) make mention of equivocation:

*Original Text version only

"O, come in, equivocator", which is thought to refer to the verbal cunning displayed by Father Garnet, one of the Gunpowder Plot conspirators in his trial of 1606. Also that year, a ship called The Tiger returned to England after a terrible two year voyage — and that ship is named in Act I Scene III (page 12*). However, as the first printed version of the play didn't appear until the Folio printing in 1623, the true dating and authenticity of each of the parts of the play are difficult to establish. For certain, a version of the play was first performed at The Globe Theatre in April 1611.

The Scottish Play

Macbeth is steeped in superstition; so much so that actors consider it the height of bad luck to even utter the name, unless they are rehearsing it at the time. Often, people will make references to "The Bard's Play" or "The Scottish Play" simply to avoid saying the "M"-word. There are a number of theories about the origins of the "curse" of Macbeth:

- It is thought that the witches' incantations are taken from real rituals and are believed to cast actual spells on the players.
- Legend has it that in 1606, Hal Berridge, the boy playing Lady Macbeth (remember that all the parts, male and female, were played by males at the time) died backstage.
- Another gruesome legend reports how in 1672 an actor playing the part of Macbeth substituted a real dagger for the blunt stage one, and actually killed the actor playing King Duncan in full view of the audience.

The more rational explanations are easier to accept.

- The majority of the play takes place in darkly lit scenes, and this tended to lead to a lot of accidents backstage.
- Yet another theory is that because Macbeth is a short play, and is so well known, that theatre groups would perform the play when they were in some financial trouble. Of course, a single play is rarely enough to save an ailing company, and therefore the performance of Macbeth became associated with failure, misery, and being out of work.

Whether any of those reasons are true or not is open to much speculation; what is beyond any doubt is that the story of Macbeth is a powerful, timeless tale of ambition, of the evil that is embedded in ill-gotten gains, and a question that lies at the heart of life itself — are we all the subjects of fate and destiny? Or do we carve out our own existence on this planet?

Page Creation

In order to create three versions of the same book, the play is first adapted into three scripts: Original Text, Plain Text and Quick Text. While the degree of complexity changes for the dialogue in each script, the artwork remains the same for all three books.

On the left is a rough thumbnail sketch of page 73 created from the script (below). Once the rough sketch is approved it is redrawn as a clean finished pencil sketch (right).

ACT 3 – SCENE 5

249. Somewhere far beyond the light of the sun, the three Witches huddle. Strange weather and strange landscapes surround them. They sense the approach of Hecate, the Queen of Darkness and they're frightened.

250. **BIG.** Suddenly she's there! Hecate appears as a triple goddess, with three heads (women's in this frame, all identical, harsh-looking, but not ugly) and three bodies, standing back-to-back. She towers over the three Witches, piercing the gloom with her fierce stare. They cringe and make frightened animal noises.

	QUICK TEXT	PLAIN ENGLISH TEXT	ORIGINAL TEXT
WITCHES (2 & 3)	WHIMPER! WHINE!	WHIMPER! WHINE!	WHIMPER! WHINE!
1ST WITCH	Hecate…you look angry.	Hecate! You look so angry.	Why, how now, Hecate! you look angerly.
HECATE	I am! You dared to meddle with Macbeth, In riddles and affairs of death,	Have I not reason, chaos that you are, Impertinent and rash? How did you dare To trade and traffic with Macbeth, In riddles, and affairs of death,	Have I not reason, beldams as you are, Saucy, and overbold? How did you dare To trade and traffic with Macbeth, In riddles, and affairs of death;

251. **BIGish.** The Witches scuttle round Hecate like dogs round their master. Hecate's three heads metamorphose into the heads of a horse, a dog and a boar.

| HECATE | You did it without me! And now I clearly see That all you've managed to do Is use him as he has used you. | And I, the mistress of your charms, The true instrument of all harms, Was never called to play my part, Or show the glory of our art? And, which is worse, all you have done Was only for a wayward son, Spiteful, and hateful; who, as others do, Wants all he can get and nought for you. | And I, the mistress of your charms, The close contriver of all harms, Was never call'd to bear my part, Or show the glory of our art? And, which is worse, all you have done Hath been but for a wayward son, Spiteful and wrathful; who, as others do, Loves for his own ends, not for you. |

From the pencil sketch an inked version of the same page is created (right).

Inking is not simply tracing over the pencil sketch, it is the process of using black ink to fill in the shaded areas and to add clarity, cohesion, depth and texture to the "pencils".

The "inks" give us the final outline which is checked for accuracy before being passed on to the colourist.

Adding colour brings the page and its characters to life.

Each character has a detailed Character Study drawn. This is useful for the artists to refer to and ensures continuity throughout the book.

Macbeth character study

The last stage of page creation is to add the speech bubbles and any sound effects.

Speech bubbles are created from the words in the script and are laid over the finished coloured artwork.

Three versions of lettering are produced for the three different versions of Macbeth. These are then saved as final artwork pages and compiled into separate books for printing.

Shakespeare Around the Globe

The Globe Theatre and Shakespeare

It is hard to appreciate today how theatres were actually a new idea in William Shakespeare's time. The very first theatre in Elizabethan London to only show plays, aptly called 'The Theatre', was introduced by an entrepreneur by the name of James Burbage. In fact, 'The Globe Theatre', possibly the most famous theatre of that era, was built from the timbers of 'The Theatre'. The landlord of 'The Theatre' was Giles Allen, who was a Puritan that disapproved of theatrical entertainment. When he decided to enforce a huge rent increase in the winter of 1598, the theatre members dismantled the building piece by piece and shipped it across the Thames to Southwark for reassembly. Allen was powerless to do anything, as the company owned the wood - although he spent three years in court trying to sue the perpetrators!

The report of the dismantling party (written by Schoenbaum) says: *"ryotous... armed... with divers and manye unlawfull and offensive weapons... in verye ryotous outragious and forcyble manner and contrarye to the lawes of your highnes Realme... and there pulling breaking and throwing downe the sayd Theater in verye outragious violent and riotous sort to the great disturbance and terrefyeing not onlye of your subjectes... but of divers others of your majesties loving subjectes there neere inhabitinge."*

William Shakespeare became a part owner of this new Globe Theatre in 1599. It was one of four major theatres in the area, along with the Swan, the Rose, and the Hope. The exact physical structure of the Globe is unknown, although scholars are fairly sure of some details through drawings from the period. The theatre itself was a closed structure with an open courtyard where the stage stood. Tiered galleries around the open area accommodated the wealthier patrons who could afford seats, and those of the lower classes - the 'groundlings' - stood around the platform or 'thrust' stage during the performance of a play. The space under and behind the stage was used for special effects, storage and costume changes. Surprisingly, although the entire structure was not very big by modern standards, it is known to have accommodated fairly large crowds - as many as 3,000 people - during a single performance.

The Globe II

In 1613, the original Globe Theatre burned to the ground when a cannon shot during a performance of "Henry VIII" set fire to the thatched roof of the gallery. Undeterred, the company completed a new Globe (this time with a tiled roof) on the foundations of its predecessor. Opened in 1614, Shakespeare didn't write any new plays for this theatre. He retired to Stratford-Upon-Avon that year, and died two years later. Despite that, performances continued until 1642, when the Puritans closed down all theatres and places of entertainment. Two years later, the Puritans razed the building to the ground in order to build tenements upon the site. No more was to be seen of the Globe for 352 years.

Shakespeare's Globe

Led by the vision of the late Sam Wanamaker, work began on the construction of a new Globe in 1993, close to the site of the original theatre. It was completed three years later, and Queen Elizabeth II officially opened the New Globe Theatre on June 12th, 1997 with a production of "Henry V".

The New Globe Theatre is as faithful a reproduction as possible to the Elizabethan theatre, given that the details of the original are only known from sketches of the time. The building can accommodate 1,500 people between the galleries and the 'groundlings.'

www.shakespeares-globe.org

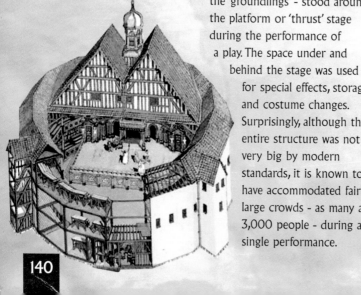

There are also replica Globe theatres in Rome and Berlin and The Old Globe in San Diego. In New York, ambitious plans are underway to convert a decaying military fortification, built to defend America against the British in the War of 1812, into a New Globe — and amazingly, the existing structure has an identical footprint to Shakespeare's Globe Theatre in London.

New Globe Theater, New York

Shakespeare Today

Our fascination with William Shakespeare has not diminished over the centuries. Despite being written over 400 years ago, his plays are still read in schools, adapted into graphic novels(!), made into films, performed in theatres the world over, and are still taken to the public by acting troupes, such as **the British Shakespeare Company**. The tradition of open-air theatre is deeply rooted in British culture. For over a thousand years companies have created theatres in the centre of towns, erecting a pageant wagon or scaffolding stage from which to perform great historical and classical drama for a mass audience. These open-air acting troupes, which weathered the theatrical shifts from medieval Mystery and Morality plays towards the sophisticated characterisation of Elizabethan drama, were the inspiration behind the British Shakespeare Company. The pageant wagons, and later inn-yards and amphitheatres outside London, were for centuries the only means by which Shakespeare and others could communicate with audiences beyond the capital. Today, more than 100,000 people watch BSC performances each year. With a full company of players and performances that feature original live music and songs, beautiful period costumes and the magic of a summer's evening, the BSC is fulfilling that primary aim of all performers throughout the years: to enchant and delight audiences of all classes and ages. **www.britishshakespearecompany.com**

The Lord Chamberlain's Men are another open-air performance troupe, with the interesting, but authentic twist that all the parts are played by men (as was the case in Shakespeare's day). **www.tcm.co.uk**

On the other side of the Atlantic, New York has Shakespeare in the Park. Since 1962, The Public Theater has staged productions of Shakespeare at The Delacorte Theater in Central Park. These performances are seen by approximately 80,000 New Yorkers and visitors each summer. In fact, since its inception, many of today's most acclaimed actors have taken part, including Patrick Stewart, Morgan Freeman, Meryl Streep, Denzel Washington, Kevin Kline and Jeff Goldblum. **www.publictheater.org**

Since 1997, Shakespeare 4 Kidz have been successfully providing an education in Shakespeare to children and young people all over the UK, and across the globe. Their unique approach has proved a hit with kids and adults alike. Their musicals have brought The Bard's work to life for thousands of people, and their creative education package is used extensively by teachers and education authorities throughout the UK. **www.shakespeare4kidz.com**

It seems that whatever time brings to our global society, and whatever developments take place within our cultures, William Shakespeare continues to have a place in our hearts and in our lives.

AVAILABLE IN THREE TEXT FORMATS

Macbeth:
The Graphic Novel
Original Text

ISBN:
978-1-906332-03-7

THE COMPLETE PLAY TRANSLATED INTO PLAIN ENGLISH!

THE FULL AND UNABRIDGED PLAY IN COMIC BOOK FORM!

Macbeth:
The Graphic Novel
Plain Text

ISBN:
978-1-906332-04-4

THE FULL STORY WITH LESS DIALOGUE FOR A FAST-PACED READ!

Macbeth:
The Graphic Novel
Quick Text

ISBN:
978-1-906332-05-1

CHOOSE FROM ONE OF THREE TEXT FORMATS, ALL USING THE SAME HIGH QUALITY ARTWORK:

Original Text

This is the full, original script -
just as The Bard intended.
This version is ideal for purists,
students and for readers
who want to experience the
unaltered text; all of the text,
all of the excitement!

Plain Text

We take the original script and
"convert" it into modern
English, verse-for-verse. If you've
ever wanted to fully
appreciate the works of
Shakespeare, but find the original
language rather cryptic, then this
is the version for you!

Quick Text

A revolution in graphic novels!
We take the dialogue and
reduce it to as few words as
possible, but still retain the
full essence of the story.
This version allows readers to
enter into and enjoy the
stories quickly.

Shakespeare's historic tale of war and peace between England and France during the reign of Henry V receives our unique and powerful treatment of being presented in a full colour graphic novel format, making it easier to absorb the plot and to immerse yourself in the story.

Experience the Battle of Agincourt as never before - and fully appreciate this decisive chapter in the history of the realm...

HENRY V: THE GRAPHIC NOVEL
Available in three text formats

Original Text

THE FULL AND UNABRIDGED PLAY IN COMIC BOOK FORM!

ISBN: 978-1-906332-00-6

Plain Text

THE COMPLETE PLAY TRANSLATED INTO PLAIN ENGLISH!

ISBN: 978-1-906332-01-3

Quick Text

THE FULL STORY WITH LESS DIALOGUE FOR A FAST-PACED READ!

ISBN: 978-1-906332-02-0

Classical Comics is a UK publisher creating graphic novel adaptations of literary classics. Faithful to the original vision of the authors, our books have been further enhanced by using only the finest artists - giving you a truly wonderful reading experience that you'll return to again and again.

Bringing Classics to Life

LOOK OUT FOR MORE TITLES IN THE CLASSICAL COMICS RANGE

Original Text
978-1-906332-06-8

Quick Text
978-1-906332-08-2

Summer 2008

Jane Eyre: The Graphic Novel

This Charlotte Brontë classic is brought to vibrant life by artist John M. Burns. His sympathetic treatment of Jane Eyre's life during the 19th century will delight any reader with its strong emotions and wonderfully rich atmosphere. Travel back to a time of grand mansions contrasted with the severest poverty and immerse yourself in this fabulous love story.

Original Text
978-1-906332-15-0

Quick Text
978-1-906332-16-7

Summer 2008

Frankenstein: The Graphic Novel

True to the original novel (rather than the square-headed Boris Karloff image from the films!) Declan Shalvey's gothic artistic style is a perfect match for this epic tale. Frankenstein is such a well known name, yet the films strayed so far beyond the original novel that many people today don't realise how this classic horror tale deals with such timeless subjects as alienation, empathy and understanding beyond appearance.

Original Text
978-1-906332-09-9

Quick Text
978-1-906332-11-2

Autumn 2008

Great Expectations: The Graphic Novel

Charles Dickens' wonderful tale of Pip, Miss Havisham, and the spiteful Estella is retold here with fresh enthusiasm contained within Victorian ambience. Told through the eyes of the main character, Pip, we follow his fortunes from boyhood to adulthood as he experiences life in the 1800s - and has a few surprises along the way!

Original Text
978-1-906332-17-4

Quick Text
978-1-906332-18-1

Autumn 2008

A Christmas Carol: The Graphic Novel

The original Christmas tale is brought to life in this colourful graphic novel adaptation. It is our second Charles Dickens title, and is probably his best-loved story. Set in Victorian England and highlighting the social injustice of the time we see one Ebeneezer Scrooge go from oppressor to benefactor when he gets a rude awakening to how his life is, and how it should be.

OUR RANGE OF CLASSICAL LITERATURE TITLES IS EXPANDING:

Romeo & Juliet		Richard III		Dracula	
Original Text	978-1-906332-19-8	Original Text	978-1-906332-22-8	Original Text	978-1-906332-25-9
Plain Text	978-1-906332-20-4	Plain Text	978-1-906332-23-5	Quick Text	978-1-906332-26-6
Quick Text	978-1-906332-21-1	Quick Text	978-1-906332-24-2		

Cover designs for illustration purposes only.

www.classicalcomics.com